James the Phisn

A Tale of a Small Phish in a World of Technology

James the Phish: A Tale of a Small Phish in a World of Technology

by Joshua Scott

Published by Scott's Capital Invesments, LLC

140A Amicks Ferry Rd. #307
Chapin, SC 29036

https://scottscap.com
Copyright © 2022 Scott's Capital Invesmtments, LLC

For permissions contact: support@scottscap.com 140A Amicks Ferry Rd. # 307 Chapin, SC 29036

ISBN: 9798351611396

Hi! I am James, a Phish.

I am small, but at certain times can create massive waves.

When I get older, I want to become the largest Phish of all time.

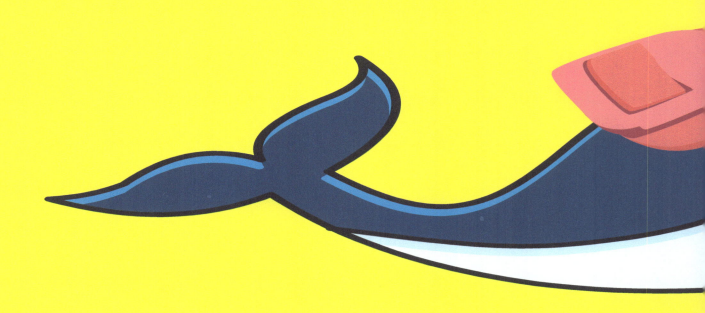

What is a phish?

Well, we start with small emails to individuals.

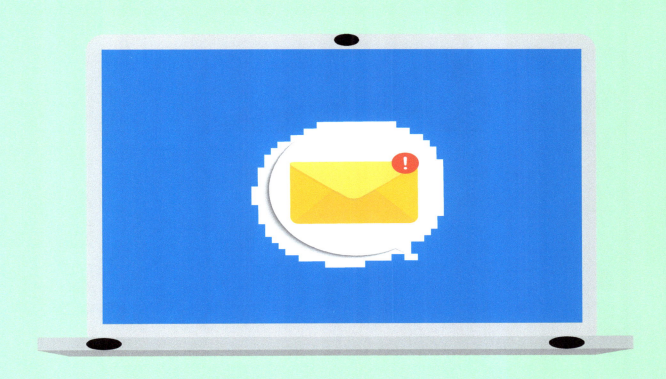

We look real but aren't real.

Hi James,

This is a reminder for ABC Comapny that Real Estate Services is moving to a new fully online

What does this mean for you?
All of your rent payments now need to be paid online through our portal.

The link to the portal is below for your convenience. Please take the time to set up your accou
pay with ease.

https://www.payment-details-info.com/make-a-payment

If you have any questions or concerns during this process. please send a message to our cust

Thank you.
 Real Estate Services

m.

at you can

ervice team.

We have fake-looking email addresses.

From: Real Estate Service <payment@estates-management.net>
Reply-To: Real Estate Services <payment@estates-management.net>
Subject: Business rent payments

Hi James,

This is a reminder for ABC Comapny that Real Estate Services is moving to a new fully on

What does this mean for you?
All of your rent payments now need to be paid online through our portal.

The link to the portal is below for your convenience. Please take the time to set up your acc
pay with ease.

https://www.payment-details-info.com/make-a-payment

If you have any questions or concerns during this process, please send a message to our o

Thank you.
 Real Estate Services

atform.

so that you can

er service team.

We might have some spelling or grammar errors.

From: Real Estate Service <payment@estates-management.net>
Reply-To: Real Estate Services <payment@estates-management.net>
Subject: Business rent payments

Hi James,

This is a reminder for ABC Comapny that Real Estate Services is mo

What does this mean for you?
All of your rent payments now need to be paid online through our por

The link to the portal is below for your convenience. Please take the t
pay with ease.

https://www.payment-details-info.com/make-a-payment

If you have any questions or concerns during this process, please se

Thank you,
 Real Estate Services

to a new fully online platform.

o set up your account so that you can

nassage to our customer service team.

We also might have some off-the-wall content.

From: Real Estate Service <payment@estates-management.net>
Reply-To: Real Estate Services <payment@estates-management.net>
Subject: Business rent payments

Hi James,

This is a reminder for ABC Comapny that Real Estate Services is moving to a new

What does this mean for you?
All of your rent payments now need to be paid online through our portal. You ca

The link to the portal is below for your convenience. Please take the time to set up
pay with ease.

https://www.payment-details-info.com/make-a-payment

If you have any questions or concerns during this process, please send a message

Thank you.
Real Estate Services

online platform.

buy more shoes

account so that you can

customer service team.

Most important!

We have fake attachments and fake hyperlinks that look like real pages that aren't. All to get you to either click on it to input information or to install a fake program on your computer.

From: Real Estate Service <payment@estates-management.net>
Reply-To: Real Estate Services <payment@estates-management.net>
Subject: Business rent payments

Hi James,

This is a reminder for ABC Comapny that Real Estate Services is moving to a new fully onlin

What does this mean for you?
All of your rent payments now need to be paid online through our portal.

The link to the portal is below for your convenience. Please take the time to set up your accou
pay with ease.

https://www.payment-details-info.com/make-a-payment

If you have any questions or concerns during this process, please send a message to our cus

Thank you.
Real Estate Services

orm.

hat you can

service team.

Once we get information, we either sell it for big money or input a virus on your computer that locks it up!

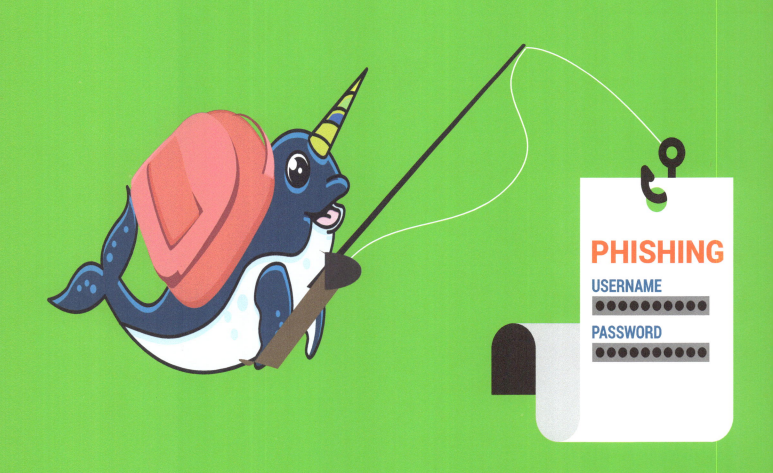

This virus that locks up your computer is Ransom ware. We make you pay a large sum to give you the keys to unlock your computer.

Therefore, I want to be the biggest Phish! I can get lots of money and fly high in the sky!

www.ingramcontent.com/pod-product-compliance
Lightning Source LLC
LaVergne TN
LVHW060202050326
832903LV00016B/351